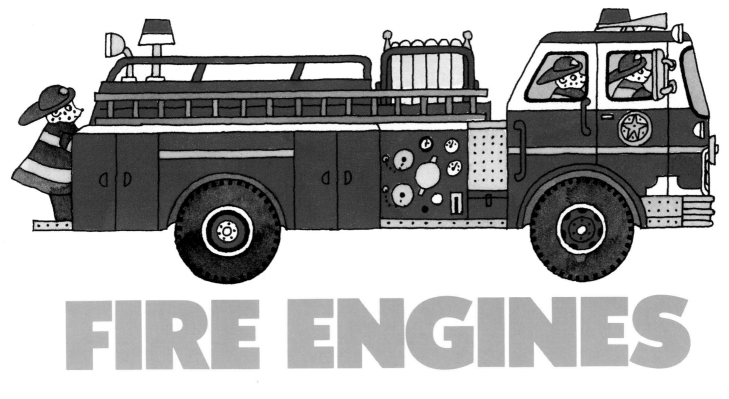

FIRE ENGINES

by Anne Rockwell

Dutton Children's Books • New York

Published by arrangement with Dutton Children's Books,
A division of Penguin Books, Inc., U.S.A.
375 Hudson Street, New York, New York, 10014

Editor: Ann Durell Designer: Isabel Warren-Lynch
Printed in the U.S.A.
COBE 10

Library of Congress Cataloging in Publication Data

Rockwell, Anne F.
  Fire engines.

  Summary: A child describes the parts of a fire
engine and how the fire fighters use them to fight fires.
  1. Fire engines—Juvenile works. 2. Fire fighters—
Juvenile works. [1. Fire engines. 2. Fire fighters]
1. Title.
TH9372.R63 1986 628.9'25 86-4464

I like fire engines.

I like to watch the fire fighters

wash and polish their fire engines.

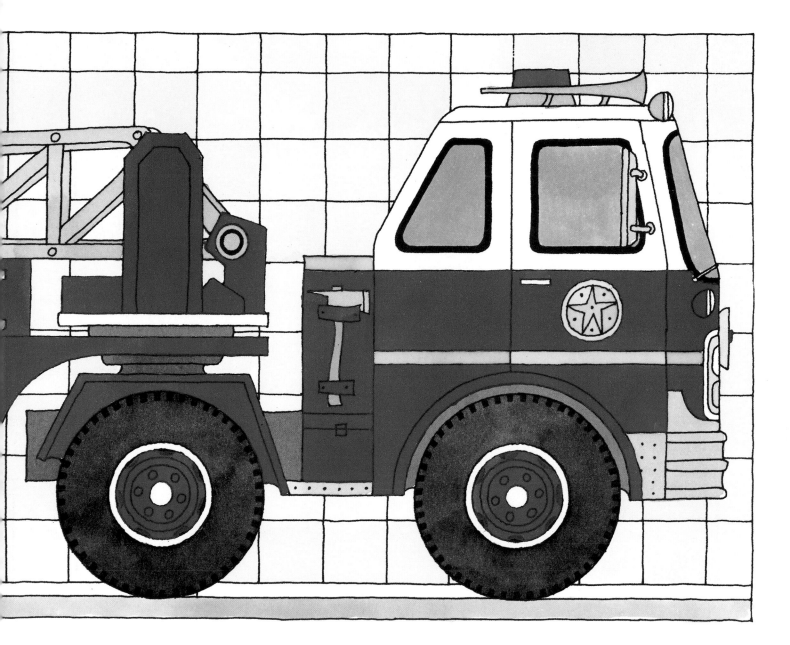

Ladder trucks have long ladders.

Motors raise the ladders high in the air.

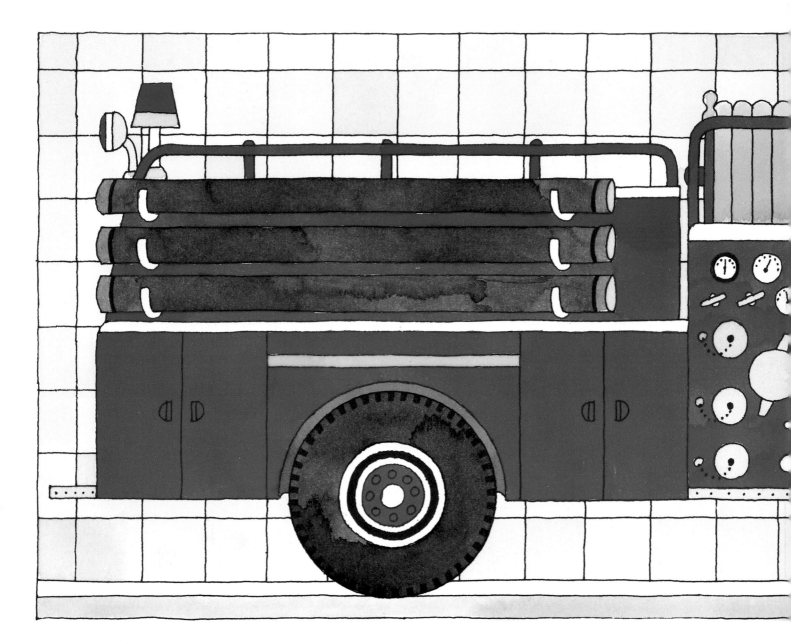

Pumper trucks have hoses and pumps.

Water is pumped from a hydrant.

Hoses spray the water on fires.

Some fire engines have pumps

and hoses and ladders.

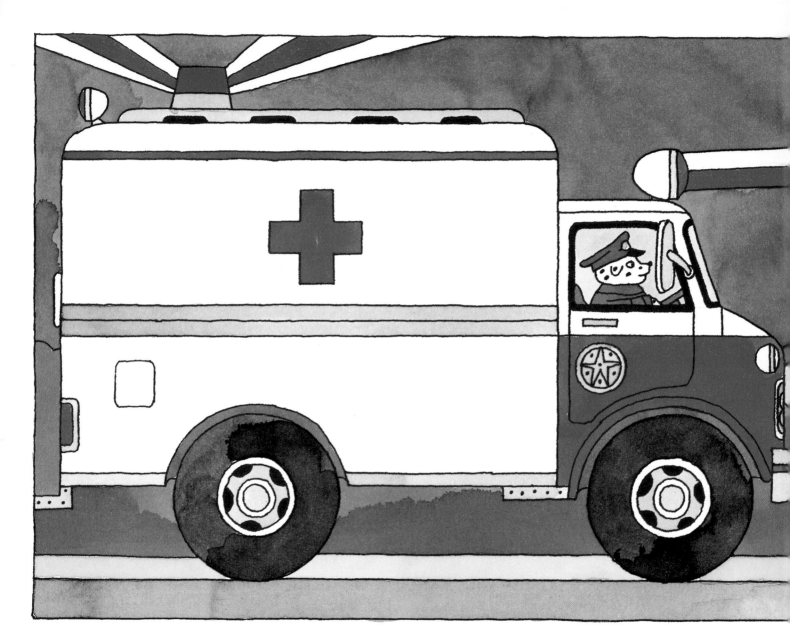

A firehouse ambulance comes
to help anyone who is hurt in a fire.

The fire chief drives a bright red car
and wears a white helmet and coat.

Some fire engines are yellow,

but I like red ones best.

Some fire engines are boats that
put out fires on ships and docks.

They spray water from the harbor.

Fire fighters are brave and strong.

Their fire engines are shiny and beautiful.

I want to be a fire fighter and drive
a real fire engine when I grow up.